To Amber Saraswati, Topaz Parvati, Metta Ganga, and Jaya Jamuna

MANDALA
PUBLISHING

Mandala Publishing
17 Paul Drive
San Rafael, CA 94903
www.mandala.org
800.688.2218

Publisher & Creative Director: Raoul Goff
Executive Directors: Michael Madden, Peter Beren
Art Director: Iain Morris
Graphic Designer: Barbara Genetin
Acquiring Editor: Lisa Fitzpatrick
Executive Editor: Mariah Bear
Project Editor: Jennifer Vetter
Design Assistance: Monika Lasiewski
Studio Production: Noah Potkin
Special thanks to Laila Williamson of the American Museum of Natural History in New York.

Library of Congress Cataloging-in-Publication Data available.

ISBN 1-60109-100-1

americanforests.org
GLOBAL
RELEAF

Palace Press International, in association with Global ReLeaf, will plant two trees for each tree used in the manufacturing of this book.
Global ReLeaf is an international campaign by American Forests, the nation's oldest nonprofit conservation organization and a world leader
in planting trees for environmental restoration.
REPLANTED PAPER

Printed in China by Palace Press International
www.palacepress.com

10 9 8 7 6 5 4 3 2 1

IN SEARCH OF THE
THUNDER DRAGON

Written and Illustrated by

Sophie & Romio Shrestha

MANDALA
PUBLISHING

"Where are we going?"
Amber asked her father.
"To the land of the Thunder Dragon," he replied.
"Where is that?" she asked.
"You will see, my love.
You will see," he answered.

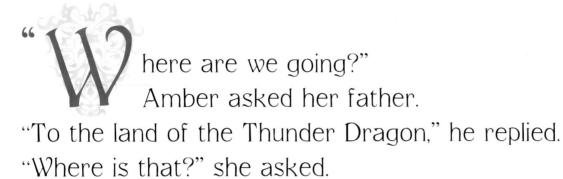

The plane taxied down the runway like a massive metal bird and took off over the hills ringing the Kathmandu Valley. Amber felt a tingle of excitement in her tummy. The white snowcaps of the mighty Himalayas pointed and glistened in the sun, etched against the bluest blue sky. Then she spotted it. "Oh look, Daddy!" Amber said. "There is Mount Everest, the highest mountain in the world." Before long, the hum of the engines lulled Amber to sleep.

Amber woke when the plane landed with a bump and the tires squealed. The brakes came on and the plane slowed down. A sign over the airport door said "Welcome to Bhutan." Before long Amber and her father were bouncing along narrow twisted roads. People waved and small children chased the car. The clouds seemed to reach gently out of the sky and gracefully curl around the mountains, as if to bless them.

Amber's cousin Tashi lived with his parents and grandfather in a Bhutanese house carved and painted with images of tigers, flowers and rainbows. Amber and Tashi's grandfather was as old as the hills, with a grey curling beard and twinkling brown eyes. His grandchildren liked to hear him tell stories by the flickering firelight at night. During big winter storms, as the thunder and lightning crashed above, he told them that they should not worry because it was just the Thunder Dragons playing hide-and-seek in the clouds.

Amber and Tashi longed to see the Thunder Dragons, so they asked their grandfather. He pondered a minute, pulling at his beard. "My little Amber and Tashi, to see the Thunder Dragons is very difficult. The only person who knows how to find them is the oldest monk in the land. He lives in a monastery far away." Tashi saddled up his mountain pony and the two cousins set off across the countryside, galloping past many villages, up hills, down hills, into forests and along wide, twisting green rivers.

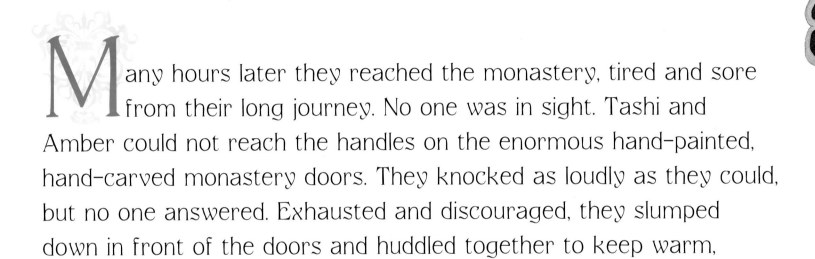

Many hours later they reached the monastery, tired and sore from their long journey. No one was in sight. Tashi and Amber could not reach the handles on the enormous hand-painted, hand-carved monastery doors. They knocked as loudly as they could, but no one answered. Exhausted and discouraged, they slumped down in front of the doors and huddled together to keep warm, wondering what had made them come so far from home.

Suddenly the door opened behind them, and they both fell backwards. They found themselves looking up at a young monk with a shaved head and saffron-yellow robes. He helped them stand up and straighten their clothes. Amber stood close to Tashi, feeling nervous and shy. "Can I help you?" asked the monk.

Tashi said, "Yes please, Lama, sir, we want to talk to the oldest monk in the monastery." Silently the monk led them along a candlelit corridor hung with images of dancing goddesses, fearsome wrathful figures, shining Buddhas and mystical scenes.

When Amber and Tashi saw the head lama, they knelt and bowed their heads to show respect. Tashi asked, "Oh please, most respected one, where can we find the Thunder Dragons?"

The lama put down his prayer book and slowly replied, "My child, I do not know where the Thunder Dragons are." The children glanced at each other in dismay. But then the lama continued, "There is a place high up in the mountains called the Tiger's Nest, home of a flying tiger. I believe she knows where the Thunder Dragons live." The lama closed his eyes and began chanting, "Oh Mane Padma Hum" over and over until the monastery walls began to vibrate with energy. Putting their hands together, quietly thanking him, the children backed out and took their leave.

Without hesitation, they began their journey towards the Tiger's Nest. Higher and higher they climbed, following a small path twisting precariously along a cliff sprigged with wild flowers and herbs. Rounding a bend in the road, they came upon a tiger with the wings of an eagle. She growled deeply and asked, "Why have you come here?"

Tashi explained, "Oh, most beautiful, strong flying Tiger, we are looking for the Thunder Dragons, and we were told by the oldest monk in the monastery that you know where they hide."

Pulling herself up to her full height, she shivered, and her striped fur rippled like waves. Nervously, the children pulled back. Her whole body started vibrating, and rainbows started twirling out of her in an aura all around her body. Mystical music seemed to come from the mountain all around, echoing, growing louder and louder. It seemed as if the whole world were humming to a celestial rhythm. As the colors faded away, she shook herself and growled, "Climb on my back, and we will find the Thunder Dragons."

Delighted, the children clambered up on the Tiger's back. Tashi wrapped his arms around her neck and Amber clung on behind. With a big roar, she took off from the cliff ledge and sailed over the patchwork of fields dotted with tiny Bhutanese houses below. Flapping her massive celestial wings, she drove through the air with powerful motions, pushing them higher and higher into the heavens. As they climbed into the clouds and the air got colder, tiny drops of condensation clung to their hair and ran down their necks, but they were too excited to notice or mind.

Thick clouds gathered, until suddenly the air lit up as two enormous dragons flew towards them. The dragons wrestled and twisted playfully as they thundered and crashed through the atmosphere like wonderful, out-of-control puppies celebrating their freedom. Dancing in ecstasy, they playfully swooped around the children on the Tiger's back. Their scales brushed the children's skin refreshingly. Their energy embraced the children, and Tashi and Amber were not afraid.

Letting go of the Tiger's fur, they stretched out their arms towards the heavens, embracing the magical air all around them. Then the Dragons roared and the rain poured down in a million pearls, bouncing off the children's skin and massaging them all over. The children knew they would never forget this night.

Exhausted and soaked but happy, the children descended with the Tiger through the clouds and landed back in her nest. They feasted on wild fruit and berries while the Tiger told them stories and answered their questions. She invited them to come back to visit her in her nest some day.

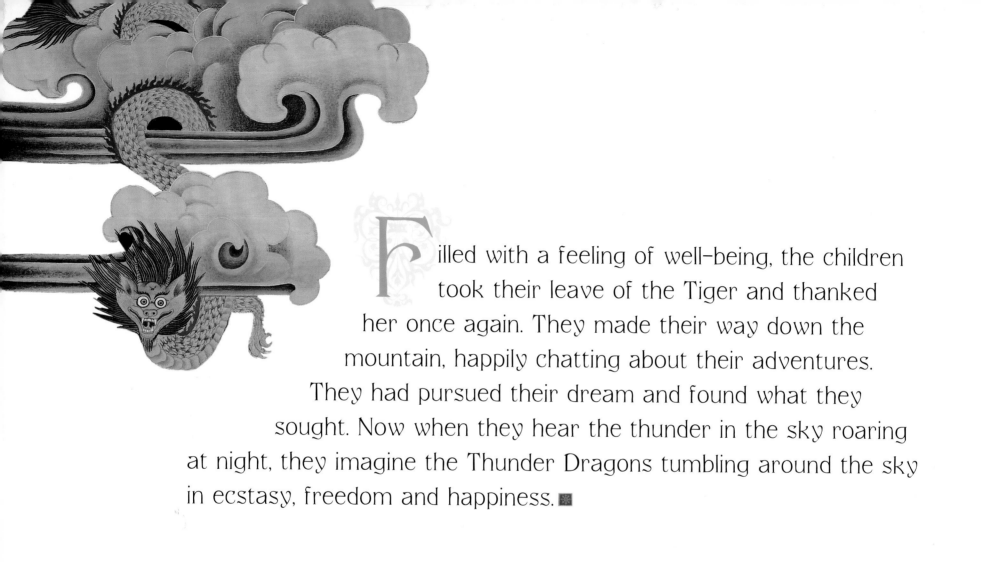

Filled with a feeling of well-being, the children took their leave of the Tiger and thanked her once again. They made their way down the mountain, happily chatting about their adventures. They had pursued their dream and found what they sought. Now when they hear the thunder in the sky roaring at night, they imagine the Thunder Dragons tumbling around the sky in ecstasy, freedom and happiness.

About Bhutan

Imagine a land in the foothills of the mighty Himalayan mountain range in Asia where clear rivers run down valleys separated by mountains, where forests and wild animals are protected, and handsome, friendly people wear colorful native dress with silver and turquoise jewelry.

Such a land is the remote Buddhist Kingdom of Bhutan. About the size of Switzerland, squeezed between the snow-capped mountains of Tibet to the north and the thick, steamy jungle in India to the south, Bhutan is naturally isolated from the rest of the world. Tigers, snow leopards, blue sheep, red pandas, and black-necked cranes still roam Bhutan, thanks to its geographical isolation and the Buddhist religion, which does not allow killing animals.

Most of the about 700,000 Bhutanese live in small farming villages with their farm animals: yaks, goats, and sheep. The people live in traditional extended families with grandparents, parents, and children in one wooden house. Most of the houses are beautifully carved with floral and mythical animal designs painted in bright colors.

Hundreds of Buddhist monasteries, some perched on steep mountainsides are home to red-robed monks and lamas (religious masters) who carry on the ancient teachings and rituals of Tibetan Buddhism. Bhutanese families encourage at least one son to become a monk in a monastery.

Bhutan is ruled by a king and a national assembly. The present king, whose father and grandfather were king before him, has proclaimed that "gross national happiness is more important than gross national product."

About this book

Amber is a real girl, the daughter of author-illustrators Sophie and Romio Shrestha. This book was inspired by her trip to her father's homeland of Nepal, and by the beauty of the land, the people, and the storytelling and artistic traditions of Bhutan. All proceeds from this book will be donated to children's charities around the world, with the intention of teaching children the importance of sharing.

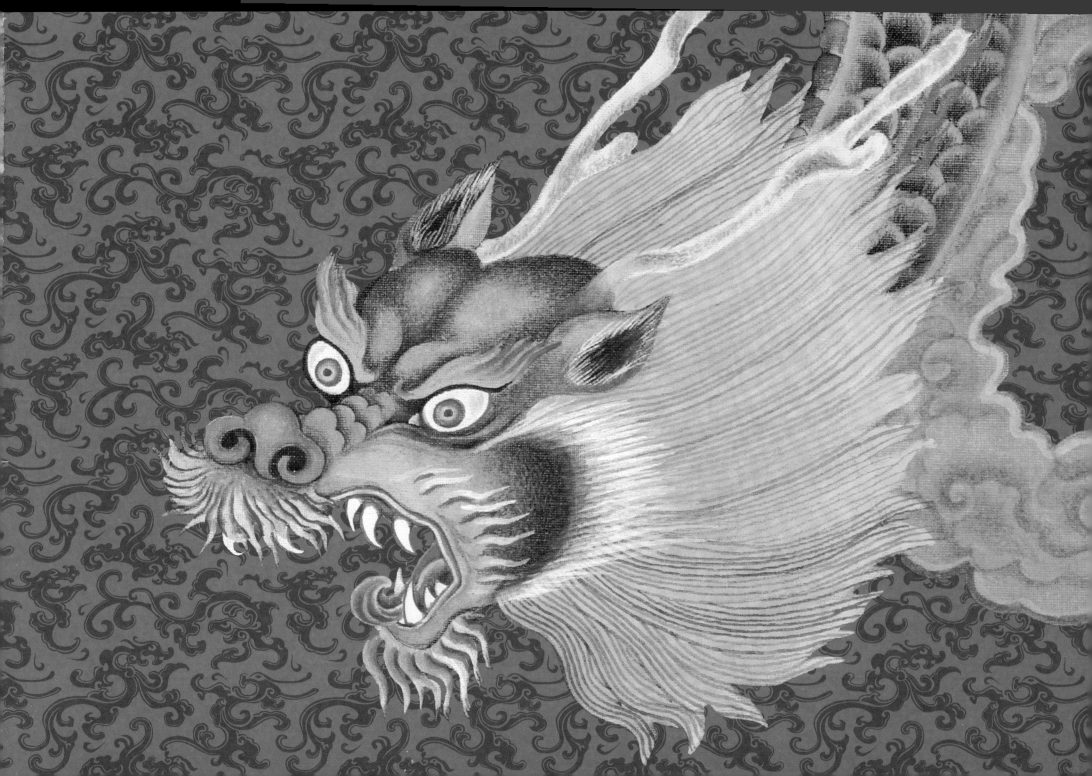

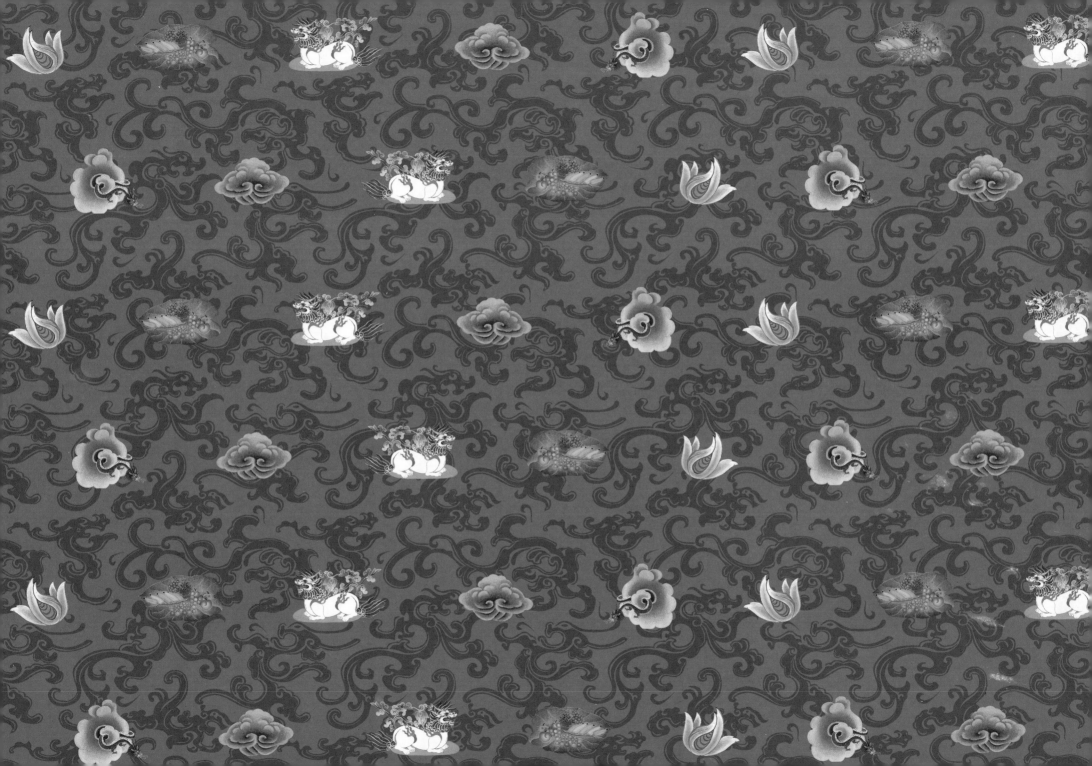